cl🍀verleaf books™

Where I Live

This Is My State

Lisa Bullard

illustrated by Holli Conger

M MILLBROOK PRESS · MINNEAPOLIS

For Dad and the Texas Bullards —L.B.

Dedicated to my elementary years in
Mesquite, Texas —H.C.

Millbrook Press
A division of Lerner Publishing Group, Inc.
241 First Avenue North
Minneapolis, MN 55401 USA

For reading levels and more information, look up this title at
www.lernerbooks.com.

Main body text set in Slappy Inline 18/28.
Typeface provided by T26.

Library of Congress Cataloging-in-Publication Data

Names: Bullard, Lisa, author. | Conger, Holli, illustrator.
Title: This is my state / by Lisa Bullard ; illustrator, Holli Conger.
Description: Minneapolis, MN : Millbrook Press, a division of Lerner
    Publishing Group, Inc. 2017. | Series: Cloverleaf books. Where I
    live | Includes bibliographical references and index.
Identifiers: LCCN 2015048982| ISBN 9781467795234 (lb : alk.
    paper) | ISBN 9781467797399 (pb : alk. paper)
Subjects: LCSH: U.S. states—Miscellanea—Juvenile literature. |
    Quarter-dollar—Collectors and collecting—Juvenile literature.
Classification: LCC E180 .B85 2017 | DDC 973—dc23

LC record available at http://lccn.loc.gov/2015048982

Manufactured in the United States of America
1-38722-20636-4/6/2016

TABLE OF CONTENTS

Chapter One

Collecting Quarters

"I got Rhode Island!" says Carlos.
"What did you get, Camila?"

"Illinois!" I answer.

A state is part of a country. States have borders and their own governments. The United States has special quarters for all fifty states.

PRETZELS

LOLLIPOPS

We're going to see Granddad in Louisiana. To get there, we have to drive across part of Texas! Mom and Dad said we have to stay out of trouble on the long drive. So we're collecting state quarters! Every time we stop for gas or food, we try to get more.

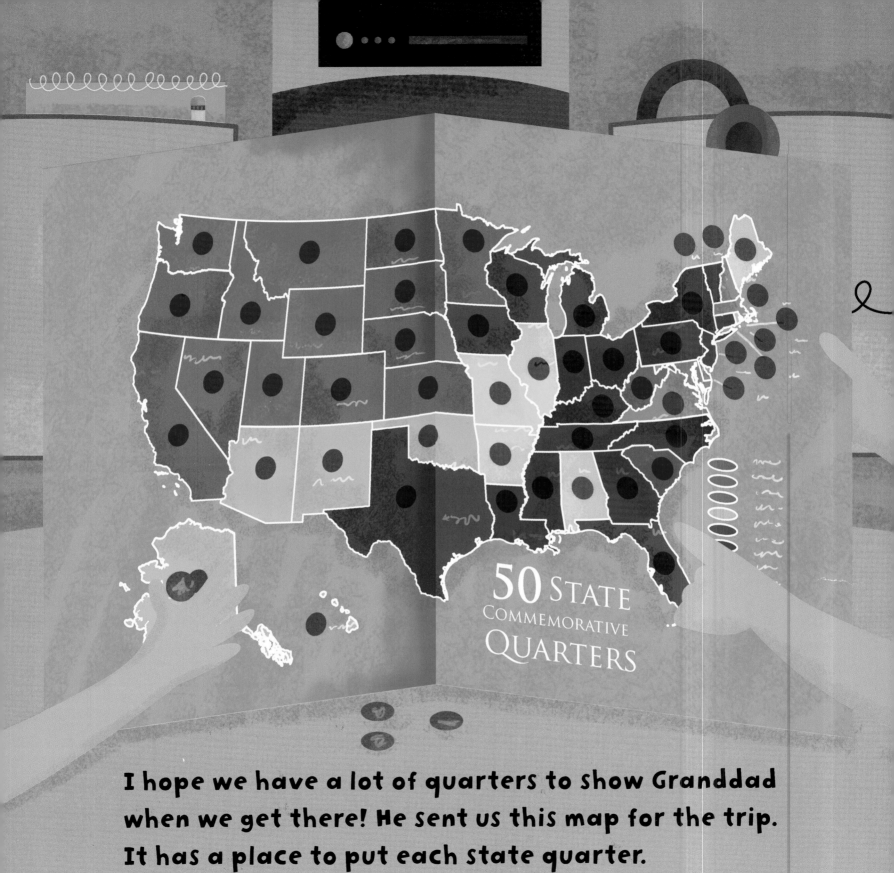

I hope we have a lot of quarters to show Granddad
when we get there! He sent us this map for the trip.
It has a place to put each state quarter.

Alaska

Rhode Island

Mom and Dad read about each state when we put its quarter in place. Dad tells us that Rhode Island is the smallest state and Alaska is the biggest state.

Each state quarter has different pictures on it. The pictures show what a state is known for, like the state flower, bird, or tree.

7

The United States started with thirteen states: Delaware, Pennsylvania, New Jersey, Georgia, Connecticut, Massachusetts, Maryland, South Carolina, New Hampshire, Virginia, New York, North Carolina, and Rhode Island.

Dad says big or small, every state in the United States is equal. He tells us the different states are kind of like me and Carlos.

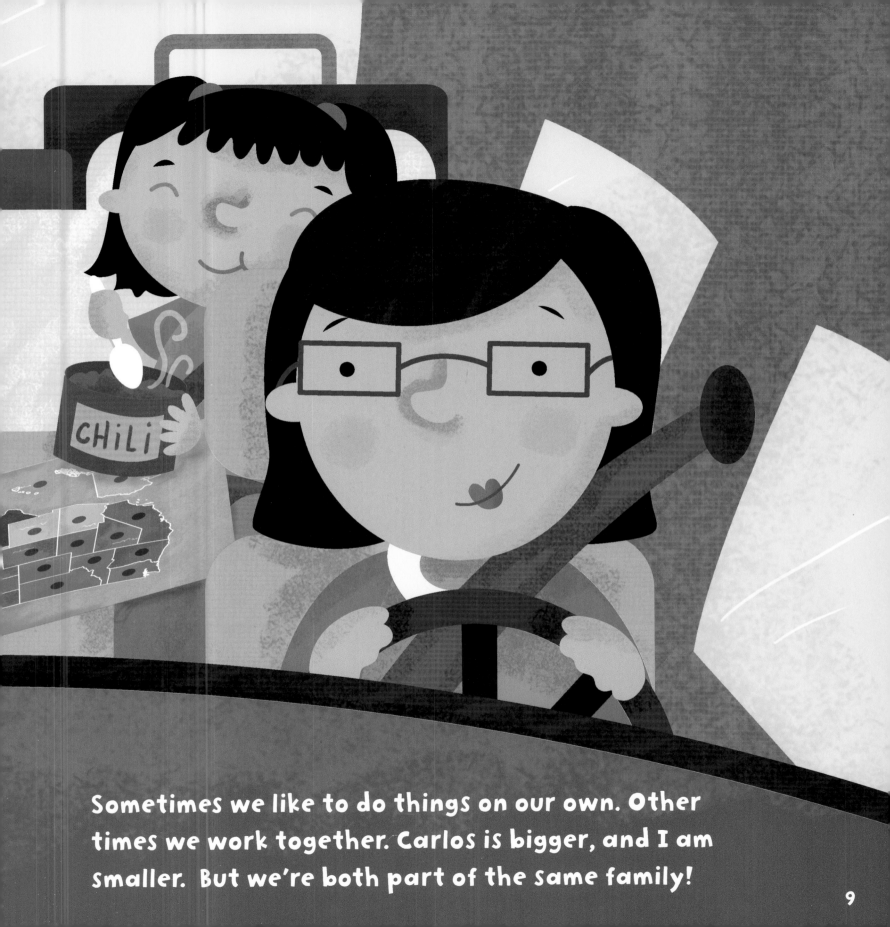

Sometimes we like to do things on our own. Other times we work together. Carlos is bigger, and I am smaller. But we're both part of the same family!

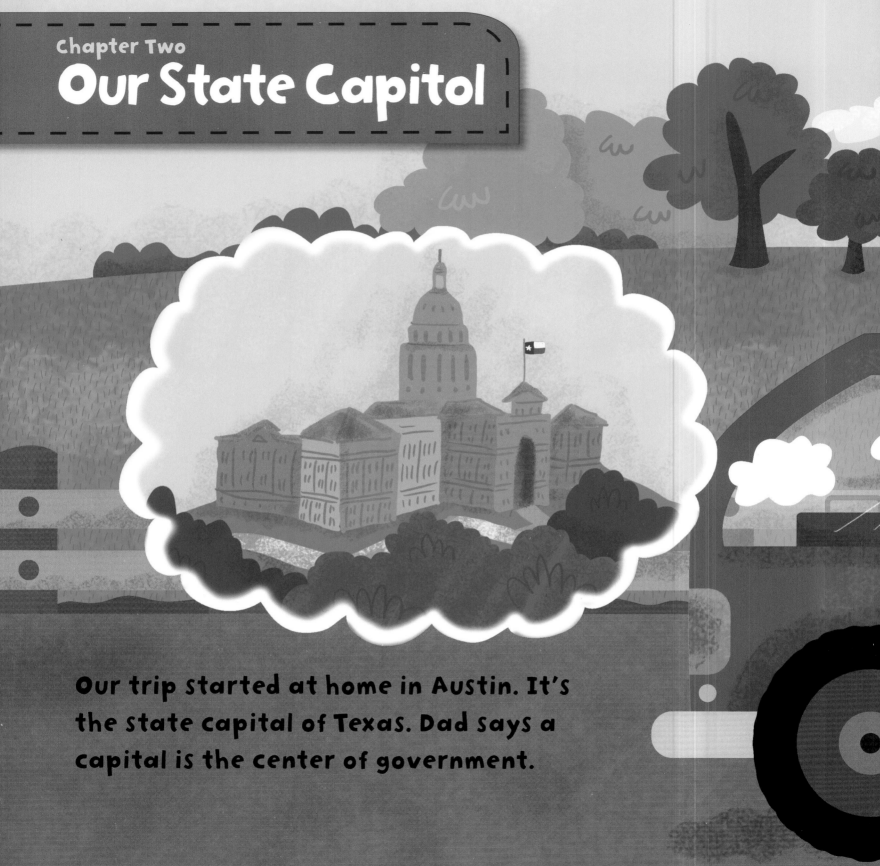

Chapter Two

Our State Capitol

Our trip started at home in Austin. It's the state capital of Texas. Dad says a capital is the center of government.

Mom works for the Texas governor. The governor is the state leader. His office is in the state capitol building. Don't you think the building looks like a castle?

Every state has a state capital and a governor. The governor is chosen by the people who live in that state.

The people who make Texas laws work in the capitol building too. At my house, Mom and Dad make the rules. Then the kids have to follow them. But even grown-ups have to follow state laws!

Dad says other state workers work all over
Texas—like a park ranger at a state park
or the crew fixing the highway.

Chapter Three

Different States

We have fifteen quarters now! We're learning a lot about different states. Here are some of my favorite facts:

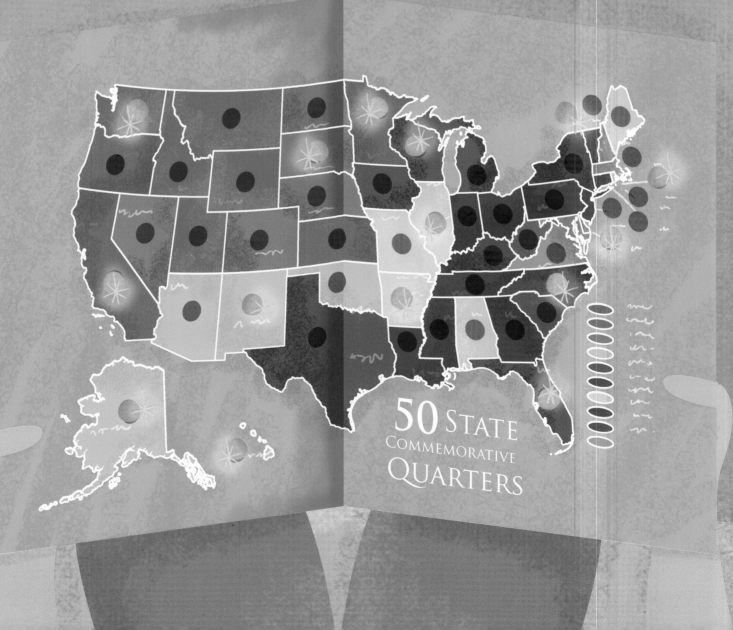

50 STATE COMMEMORATIVE QUARTERS

The alligator is Florida's official state reptile.

Aloha means both "hello" and "good-bye" in Hawaii.

Four presidents' faces are carved on Mount Rushmore in South Dakota.

Washington produces more apples than any other state.

Minnesota has 11,842 lakes.

"Take a look!" Mom says. Dad points to a sign.
It says, "Louisiana State Line."

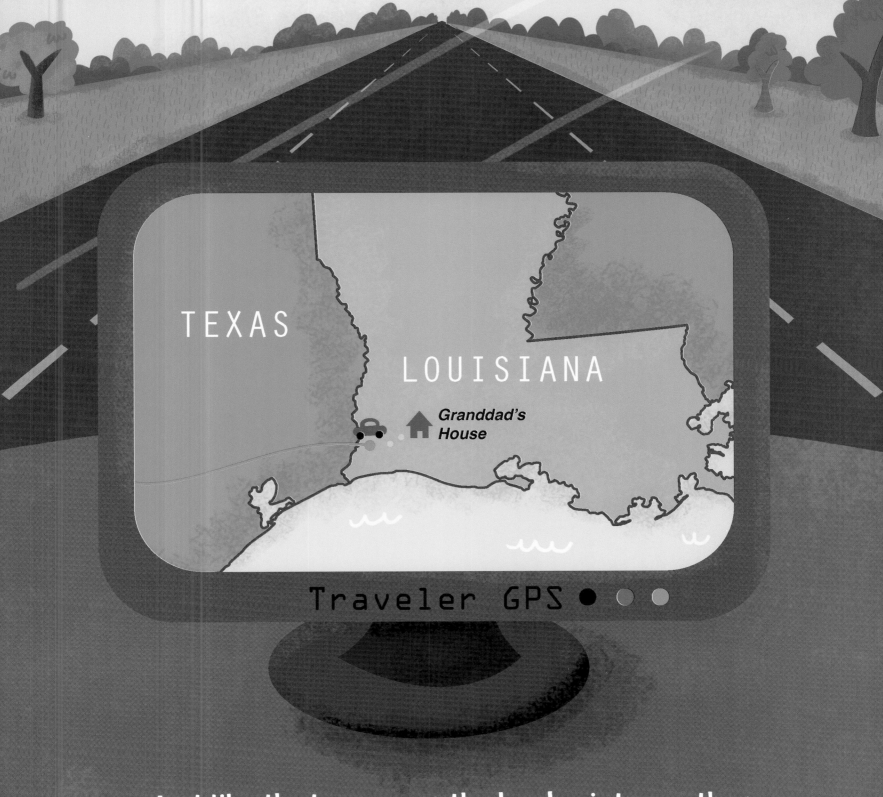

Just like that, we cross the border into another state! We're almost to Granddad's house!

Chapter Four

Texas in My Pocket

We have nineteen quarters, but we're still missing Texas. But even without that quarter, we've seen a lot of Texas today!

Maybe someday, I can visit all fifty states. Mom says I could stand on four states at once at the Four Corners Monument!

Four states meet at Four Corners Monument. They are Arizona, Colorado, New Mexico, and Utah.

Granddad comes out to hug us when we pull into his driveway. "Close your eyes and hold out your hands," he says. Then, "Open!"

I look down and see a Texas state quarter.
Carlos gets one too. Granddad even has an
extra to put in our US map. We're going to
have lots of fun in Louisiana. But I'm going
to carry my state in my pocket while we do!

State Map Hunt

Camila and Carlos traveled a long way to visit Granddad. Can you find the places they talked about on the map below? Can you find these same places in the story's pictures too?

- Austin, Texas

- Louisiana

- Granddad's house

- Four Corners Monument

GLOSSARY

border: the outside edge of a state or country

capital: the center of government

capitol: the building where the people who make the laws work

country: a nation made up of land and people with a government

government: a set of rules that a group must live by and the people who make those rules

governor: the leader of a state

law: a rule of a government

state: an area that has borders and its own government and is part of a larger country

state line: a state border that appears as a line on a map

TO LEARN MORE

BOOKS
Bullard, Lisa. *This Is My Country.* Minneapolis: Millbrook, 2017.
Now that you've learned about states, learn about countries in this fun book!

Machajewski, Sarah. *What Are State and Local Governments?* New York: Britannica, 2016.
Read this book to learn more about how state government works.

National Geographic Society. *Beginner's United States Atlas.* Des Moines: National Geographic Children's Books, 2009.
The information, photographs, and maps in this book will teach you interesting facts about each of the fifty states.

WEBSITES
50 State Quarters® Program
http://www.usmint.gov/kids/coinNews/50sq
See all the different state quarters and play games at this website.

USA for Kids
http://www.usconsulate.org.hk/pas/kids/50states.htm
This website lets you explore facts about each of the fifty states.

US State Games
http://www.learninggamesforkids.com/us-state-games.html
Visit this website to find games for each of the fifty states.

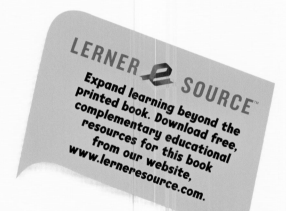

LERNER SOURCE™
Expand learning beyond the printed book. Download free, complementary educational resources for this book from our website, www.lerneresource.com.

INDEX